LET'S TALK STRAIGHT!

Queer Stories From Indian Mythology

Priyanka Seth

INDIA • SINGAPORE • MALAYSIA

ISBN

Hardcase 979-8-89744-011-5
Paperback 979-8-89744-010-8

To my ***Papa,*** whose silent wisdom and steadfast love continue to guide me, and whose absence is a presence I carry with me always.

Your memory reminds me that life's stories, like our souls, are eternal. This book is for you, who taught me to cherish the power of storytelling and to see divinity in the unexpected.

न जायते म्रियते वा कदाचित्
नायं भूत्वा भविता वा न भूयः।
अजो नित्यः शाश्वतोऽयं पुराणो
न हन्यते हन्यमाने शरीरे॥

"The soul is never born, nor does it die. It is not slain when the body is slain."

– Bhagavad Gita

(Chapter 2, Verse 20)

This book is dedicated to all those who dare to explore the depths of ancient Indian mythology, to those who find beauty in the fluidity of gender roles, and to those who embrace the enduring power of stories to teach us about ourselves and the world around us. May this exploration inspire you to challenge conventional narratives, question assumptions, and embrace the myriad possibilities of love and family.

Contents

Prologue

"*Let's Talk Straight*" isn't just a book—it's an invitation to peek behind the curtains of ancient Indian mythology and discover the lesser-known, wonderfully complex relationships hidden in the Vedic and Puranic texts. Think of it as a friendly nudge to see these age-old stories in a fresh, modern light, uncovering layers of meaning that might have been conveniently tucked away over centuries.

This isn't about poking holes in tradition; it's about zooming out and asking: "Wait, what if there's more to this?" It's about challenging rigid interpretations of love, family, and identities that have been handed down unquestioned. Ancient Indian mythology, for all its patriarchal packaging, has these surprising gems—hints of gender fluidity, diverse love, and an openness that feels downright ahead of its time.

Through the lens of relationships like *Mitra-Varuna* or *Chandra-Mala*, the dual identity of *Harihara*, or the story of *Shikhandini*, this book delves into possibilities that traditional readings often skip over. Were these stories only about cosmic partnerships, divine brotherhood, or duality? Or could they also be about intimate bonds, same-sex connections, or queer identities?

This book doesn't claim to have all the answers (because, let's be honest, mythology thrives in its mystery). But it does make us ask the questions—and maybe that's where the magic lies.

So, here's the deal: this isn't just a journey through myths. It's an exploration of how these ancient tales still resonate today, challenging norms and expanding our understanding of love, gender, and the messy, beautiful human experience. Let's dive in together, shall we?

1

Divine Surrogacy

Once upon a time, when the gods still walked the earth and the sky had no end, there were two very, very good friends named Mitra and Varuna. These two weren't just your average *"text each other memes"* kind of friends—they were the ultimate cosmic duo. Imagine a pair of deities so in sync they could finish each other's prayers, steal each other's snacks, and know precisely what the other is thinking when they raised a single eyebrow. Like a morse code of the face, only with some hair and skin.

They ruled over the winds, rivers and seas, ensuring the air and waters stayed calm, the tides danced on command, and the mortals didn't turn the Earth into a soggy disaster. Their friendship was legendary, and they were known to ride the heavens together in a chariot pulled by seven swans—because walking is for mere mortals, and swans are clearly the Rolls-Royce of mythology.

The palace they called home? Golden walls that shimmered even in waning moonlight, grand diwans that were stacked with silk cushions embroidered with constellations, and chandeliers dripping diamonds that seemed to be hanging directly from the sky. A palace so grand, it made Versailles look like a shabby, old hut.

Their palace had a thousand pillars—each carved with intricate stories of their exploits—and a thousand doors, which sounds like a security nightmare, but when you're a god, you can afford that kind of architectural drama. Inside, they lounged around on plush silks, draped in jewels that sparkled like stars, and basically epitomized glamor. These weren't just any gods; they were the lords of the rivers and seas, guardians of the entire world, and together they kept everything flowing smoothly—like a divine tag team.

"Varuna, you left your anklet on the third staircase again," Mitra teased one morning as he lounged on a velvet couch, flipping through scrolls of gossip.

Varuna smirked, adjusting his sapphire-studded crown. *"And you've been borrowing my emerald bracelets without asking. We're even."*

Their banter flowed as easily as the air and rivers they governed. Life was perfect.

Now, here's the kicker: Mitra and Varuna were more than just friends. Their friendship was so strong, they decided to become parents together. Yes, you read that right. These two gods, despite the fact that traditional biology wasn't exactly on their side, somehow managed to father not one but two children together. And those kids didn't just grow up to be anyone—they became Rishi Agastya and Rishi Vashishtha, two of the most famous sages in the history of sages.

You can imagine the celestial gossip this must have stirred up. *"Did you hear? Mitra and Varuna—together! And with kids, no less!"* Their story was passed down, whispered, and argued over for centuries. Some said that Mitra and Varuna were more like two halves of a single soul, but others saw it differently. The tales of their relationship were peppered throughout sacred texts like the Rigveda, the Matsya Purana, and the Bhagavad Purana. According to the latter, their unconventional family story began in the strangest of ways.

It all started when Indra, the king of the gods (the hierarchy of gods is a big chaotic thing of its own) and notorious troublemaker, spotted two rishis—Nara and Narayana—sitting deep in meditation on the Gandhamadana Mountain. Now, Indra had this little habit of panicking whenever he saw anyone getting too spiritually powerful. Heaven forbid someone might get more powerful than him. So he hatched a plan and sent a gaggle of Apsaras—the celestial dancers—to go and distract the meditating rishis. Decked out in the finest of their bling wear that shone like the Milky Way, the Apsaras danced, sang, and generally did everything in their power to throw off the rishis' concentration. But Narayana, being the clever sage he was, saw right through Indra's little scheme. *"Indra, you've got to try harder,"* he muttered. Instead of shooing the Apsaras away, he calmly created a woman so incredibly beautiful, so beyond anything the Apsaras could imagine, that they all froze mid-

dance. their jewelry just like their jaws hung lifeless, their lungs deflated as the air was sucked out of the universe.

She was called Urvashi, and she was everything grace and beauty could be. The Apsaras suddenly felt like they'd been downgraded from prime time to a re-run.

Meanwhile, Mitra and Varuna, who had nothing better to do than gazing at the earthly realm from their heavenly balcony, caught sight of Urvashi. *"Is it just me, or is she glowing?"* Varuna whispered, leaning closer.

"Glowing? She's radiating," Mitra replied, his voice barely above a whisper.

They were spellbound. And when gods are spellbound, let's just say things tend to get a little... complicated. In their moment of awe, something unexpected happened...a divine *'Oops!'* moment. They were so struck by Urvashi's beauty, so overwhelmed by her radiance, that they both— how do I put this delicately—lost control of themselves. Together. At the same time. Their combined essence, their godly *"offspring starter kit,*" spilled onto the earth. It didn't land just anywhere; it pooled into a large, enchanted mud pitcher. Because, in case you didn't know, in ancient mythology, mud pitchers were like the original surrogacy method. Nine months later—or whatever the divine gestational period is—out popped two little bundles of joy: Agastya and Vashishtha.

"*Twins?*" Mitra exclaimed, holding the squirming bundles. "*We're naturals at this parenting thing!*"

Varuna chuckled, cradling the other baby. "*Looks like we've set a new standard for godly family planning.*"

Now, raising kids isn't easy—ask any mortal. But when you're Mitra and Varuna, it comes with its own set of challenges. Their palace was suddenly filled with the cries of newborns and the occasional celestial diaper dilemma.

One evening, as the babies slept, Mitra turned to Varuna. "*Do you think they'll inherit your patience or my quick temper?*"

"*Hopefully a bit of both,*" Varuna replied with a soft smile. "*Balance is everything.*"

Agastya and Vashishtha grew into legendary sages, shaping the spiritual fabric of India for centuries.

But their story wasn't just about parenthood. Mitra and Varuna's bond was deeper than any title—whether you called them best friends, partners, or two halves of one divine soul. They weren't afraid to challenge celestial norms. They ruled the heavens together, their connection unwavering, a testament to love in its purest, most transcendent form.

Riding their swan-pulled chariot, they often watched the waxing and waning moon. *"Funny how we're like the moon phases,"* Mitra mused one night.

"How so?" Varuna asked, resting his head on his palm.

"You're bold and bright, like the waxing moon. I'm quieter, like the waning phase. Together, we complete the cycle."

Varuna smiled. *"And that's why we work."*

And yet, there are those who claim Mitra and Varuna aren't two beings at all, but rather a single entity split into two personas. Which, honestly, feels like a bit of a cop-out. The Rigveda is sprinkled with hints—little winks to the reader—that they were more than just besties. Even the times when the new moon and full moon merge are deemed inauspicious for procreation—almost as if to say that such a close, same-sex bond is something truly heavenly and unique, but not meant for creating life in the usual way.

But that didn't stop Mitra and Varuna eons back. With a little help from Urvashi and the magic mud pitcher, Mitra and Varuna managed to prove that love—however unconventional—was powerful enough to transcend any boundary.

And if that's not the original story of surrogacy, I don't know what is.

So the next time someone tells you that the ancients were all about strict rules and rigid traditions, remind them about Mitra and Varuna— the two friends who loved each other so much they fathered two of the greatest sages together, without a single shred of self-doubt.

Because in the end, the gods were just as messy, complicated, and beautifully human as the rest of us.

* * * * *

2

Born of Two Mothers

You remember Sage Bhagiratha, right? The man who brought the holy Ganga down to Earth? The noble soul who meditated so fiercely that the gods had no choice but to relent? That's the story we've all been told: a tale of dedication, heroism, and divine intervention. But, if you're willing to peel back the layers of mythology, you'll find there's another side to Bhagiratha's story.

Let's put those polished, family-friendly narratives aside for a moment and delve into the origin of his name. Yes, his name. *"Bhagiratha"* isn't just a string of syllables chosen for its poetic ring. It has a very specific, and let's be honest, slightly eyebrow-raising meaning. In Sanskrit, Bhaga means… vulva. Yes, you heard that right. Why, you may wonder, was this renowned sage named after such an intimate part of the anatomy? Well, as it turns out, when your parents are a royal same-sex couple, the naming process gets a bit more... creative. The thing is Bhagiratha was born from the intimate embrace of two women, and it was Lord Brahma himself who chose the name.

Our story begins in Ayodhya, where King Dilipa of the illustrious Suryavanshi lineage ruled with wisdom and valour—until, one day, he didn't. He died, as kings do, but with one glaring problem: no heir to carry on the royal bloodline. His two queens, Chandra and Mala, were left behind to grieve in their sprawling palace, now eerily quiet.

"What do we do now?" Chandra asked Mala one evening as they sat in the gardens, watching the sunset.

Mala sighed, her voice heavy with sorrow. *"The kingdom expects an heir. But with Dilipa gone... it feels like we've failed."*

As days turned into weeks, and weeks into months, the gods began to panic. You see, the Suryavanshi lineage wasn't just any family tree—it was **the** family tree, destined to give rise to heroes like Rama. If this lineage ended, it would be a catastrophe of heavenly proportions. So, the celestial bigwigs—Brahma, Vishnu, and Shiva—called for an emergency meeting on Mount Kailash.

"Alright, folks," Brahma began, stroking his long, white beard. *"We have a problem. No heir in Ayodhya. No Suryavanshis means no Rama. Thoughts?"*

Vishnu leaned back, arms crossed, his expression thoughtful. *"What if we reincarnate Dilipa and give him a second chance?"*

Shiva snorted. *"Too much paperwork. Why don't we just… create an heir?"*

"Create one?" Vishnu raised an eyebrow. *"What, out of thin air?"*

Brahma smiled slyly. *"Not thin air. Two queens, two wombs, one solution."*

The gods stared at him in silence, and then Shiva broke into a grin. *"Bold. I like it."*

To execute this bold idea, Brahma called upon Kama, the mischievous God of Love. Now, Kama wasn't your average cherub with a bow and arrow.

He was a full-blown force of nature, capable of sparking desire in the coldest of hearts. If anyone could nudge the queens toward divine procreation, it was him.

"You need me to spark desire between two queens?" he asked, twirling his flower-tipped arrow. *"Piece of cake."*

Before Kama began his work, however, he sought out Sage Vashistha, the royal family's spiritual guide. *"Sage,"* he said with a mock bow, *"I'm about to rewrite the rules of lineage. Are you ready?"*

Vashistha's eyes narrowed. *"This is unnatural,"* he declared, his voice echoing through the hermitage.

"Unnatural?" Kama grinned. *"Says the man who's seen cows produce sages. Let's not pretend we're bound by mortal definitions here."*

Vashistha huffed but didn't object further. With the sage's half-hearted blessing, Kama set his sights on Ayodhya.

Kama arrived at the palace like he owned the place, his presence announced by a warm breeze that carried the faint scent of jasmine. The palace was quiet when Kama arrived, save for the soft rustling of rain against the windows. Chandra and Mala were in their chambers, their hearts heavy with grief. But Kama wasn't deterred.

Then, with a dramatic sigh, he muttered to himself, *"Timing is everything."*

And timing, as it happened, wasn't quite right. Both queens were menstruating. So Kama, ever the patient god, decided to bide his time. For three days, he lingered, working his magic subtly. He filled the palace gardens with blooming flowers, sent soft rains to wash the air clean, and coaxed peacocks into dancing under the clouds. By the time the queens' cycles ended, the palace was practically oozing romance.

The queens, unaware of his presence, sat side by side, gazing at the flickering lamps. *"Do you ever feel like we're just... existing?"* Chandra asked, her voice barely a whisper.

Mala reached for her hand. *"I do. But I also feel like we're stronger together."*

Kama struck in that moment. With a flick of his wrist, he released his magic, and a warmth spread through the room. The grief that had weighed them down for so long began to lift, replaced by an undeniable, burning desire for one another. As the rain poured outside, the queens found solace in each other's arms, their love transcending the boundaries of societal norms.

The next morning, Brahma showed up unannounced (classic Brahma move). *"Good news, ladies!"* he declared. *"You're going to be mothers!"*

Chandra and Mala exchanged bewildered looks. *"Uh, how?"* Chandra asked, gesturing vaguely at the lack of a man in the picture.

Mala was worried. *"What would the court say? What would the world think?"*

Desperate and terrified, she was ready to end it all.

But Brahma, our celestial problem-solver calmed Mala with his gentle words and reassurances. This, he explained, was no ordinary pregnancy; it was the will of the gods. The child she carried would be no ordinary child—he would be a hero, a sage, a man who would change the course of history. And, just in case Mala still had doubts, Brahma offered her the ultimate celestial warranty: if society found

her actions questionable, he would personally bear the consequences.

So, with a blessed guarantee in place, Mala carried the pregnancy to term.

Three trimesters later, the queens welcomed a baby boy. He was strong, healthy, and had a sparkle in his eyes that could rival the stars. The palace erupted in celebration, and the gods heaved a collective sigh of relief.

But then came the matter of naming the child. As the celestial naming committee convened, Brahma suggested *"Bhagiratha."*

Mala blinked. *"Bhagi… what?"*

"Bhagiratha," Brahma repeated, his tone firm. *"Born of extraordinary circumstances, he carries the mark of the god."*

Chandra couldn't help but laugh. *"You named our son after… vulva?"*

Brahma shrugged. *"It's poetic. He's literally the product of two wombs."*

And so, Bhagiratha grew up with a name that carried the weight of his unique origin—a name that celebrated the power of love, resilience, and defying convention. And while some might raise their eyebrows at the circumstances of his conception, the fact remains: he went on to be one of the most celebrated figures in Hindu mythology.

Of course, the official records gloss over this part of the story. Most people prefer the version where Bhagiratha is a noble sage who tamed the Ganga. But let's be real: his origin story is the real showstopper. It's a tale of love, loss, and godly meddling, proving that even in mythology, family comes in all shapes and sizes.

So the next time someone mentions Bhagiratha, feel free to drop this little tidbit: the man who brought the Ganga to Earth was also the product of a love so unconventional it left us scratching our heads.

Because in the grand, messy tapestry of myth and legend, sometimes it's the stories that don't make it into the mainstream that are the most intriguing—the ones that remind us that love, in all its forms, is a force that even the gods can't resist.

* * * * *

3

Amalgamation of Sexuality

Once upon a time, in the sprawling celestial playhouse of mythology—where gods debated, danced, and occasionally invented entire species—Lord Shiva found himself in the middle of a rather awkward conversation. Lord Brahma, the self-proclaimed Creator of the Universe, was pacing nervously. His golden complexion was unusually pale, and his four faces, usually brimming with divine confidence, wore identical expressions of sheer panic.

"Shiva," Brahma began, clearing his throats (all four of them), *"we have a situation."*

Shiva, ever the cosmic yogi, barely looked up from his meditative pose atop Mount Kailash. His matted hair glistened with ice, and his serpent coiled lazily around his neck, clearly enjoying the vibe. "*What kind of situation?*" Shiva drawled, his voice as calm as a Himalayan breeze, well, just regular breeze for Shiva.

"*Well,*" Brahma began, gesturing wildly, "*I created the Prajapatis—all strong, capable, and... well, male. I thought they'd populate the universe. But... nothing's happening. They just sit around flexing their muscles and comparing mustaches. It's like a celestial frat house with no beer or purpose.*"

For the first time, Shiva opened one eye, his expression caught somewhere between amusement and exasperation. "*Brahma,*" he said, adjusting his tiger-skin tankini, "*are you seriously telling me you thought a bunch of men would just magically... reproduce?*"

Brahma blinked, all four of his heads looking genuinely confused. "*Well... yes?*"

Shiva sighed deeply, the kind of sigh that only someone dealing with eternal cosmic incompetence could muster. "*Brahma,*" he said, his tone as patient as a teacher explaining algebra to a goldfish, "*creation requires balance. Masculine and feminine. Action and nurture. A force to complement the other. You didn't think this through, did you?*"

Brahma flushed. *"I mean, I thought it was implied…"*

Shiva smirked. *"Clearly, it wasn't."*

And because he never missed an opportunity for a theatrical lesson, Shiva decided it was time for a cosmic demonstration. The winds around Mount Kailash stilled, the skies dimmed, and a soft golden light enveloped Shiva. With a shimmer of energy and what can only be described as a divine drumroll, he transformed into Ardhanarishvara—a breathtaking fusion of masculine and feminine energies.

On his right, Shiva remained in his untamed glory: ash-smeared skin, wild dreadlocks adorned with Ganga's flowing waters, and his signature snake accessory game on point. On his left, however, he became Parvati, his consort: radiant in silken robes, bedecked in gold ornaments, her serene beauty amplified by the soft glow of the crescent moon in her hair. Together, they stood as one entity, embodying the perfect balance of yin and yang, action and compassion, creation and destruction.

Brahma's jaw dropped so fast it was a wonder it didn't break through the clouds below. *"Oh…*

OH! Now I get it!" he exclaimed, smacking his forehead. "I need a feminine force! How could I have missed something so obvious?"

Shiva raised an eyebrow, his expression clearly saying, *You're the Creator. This is literally your job.*

Suitably chastised, Brahma rushed off to Parvati to apologize profusely. *"Great Goddess,"* he began, bowing so deeply that his crowns wobbled precariously, threatening to tumble off. *"I have made a monumental oversight. Will you help me restore balance to creation?"*

Parvati, ever graceful and understanding, smiled with a glimmer of amusement. *"It seems Shiva's lesson has finally pierced through,"* she said, her tone teasing but not unkind. *"Very well, Brahma. I will help. But remember—creation is not just about function. It's about harmony, beauty, and balance."*

With a wave of her hand, she created women—wise, nurturing, and powerful beings—to complement the Prajapatis. As the universe settled into this newfound equilibrium, creation thrived, brimming with a dynamic energy.

But wait! The story of godly mergers doesn't end there. Fast forward a bit on the mythological timeline, and we find Shiva teaming up with another cosmic heavyweight: Lord Vishnu for yet another groundbreaking collaboration.

It all began during a celestial brainstorming session. Vishnu, lounging in his palace on Vaikuntha , reclined elegantly on Ananta, his serpent throne, and turned his gaze toward Kailasa. "*Shiva,*" he began, his voice smooth as honey, "*I've been thinking. You know how mortals keep debating about which of us is greater?*"

Shiva, seated cross-legged and adorned with ash, opened one eye, his expression a mix of mild curiosity and mild exasperation. "*Yes, and?*"

"*Well,*" Vishnu said, a mischievous grin spreading across his face, "*why not put this debate to rest once and for all? Let's merge. Half you, half me. The ultimate celestial collaboration.*" His golden crown caught the light like a cosmic disco ball, as though punctuating his brilliance.

Shiva arched an eyebrow, his lips curving into a smirk. "*A cosmic remix, you say? Sounds intriguing. Let's do it.*"

And with a swirl of divine energy, the two gods merged to create Harihara—a seamless union of opposites. The right half was Shiva, fierce and ascetic, clad in tiger skin and radiating the untamed power of destruction. The left half was Vishnu, resplendent in golden robes, adorned with glittering jewels, embodying preservation and harmony. Together, they formed a striking, unified deity—an embodiment of the ultimate truth that creation and destruction, chaos and order, are not adversaries but partners in the eternal dance of existence.

Of course, this new form stirred up a friendly rivalry among their followers. The Shaivites proudly declared, *"Shiva's half is obviously superior!"* The Vaishnavas countered with equal fervor, *"Clearly, Vishnu's side is the main attraction!"* Both sides conveniently ignored the entire point of Harihara: to demonstrate that the two were equal facets of the same supreme reality.

And yet, the story doesn't stop there. Through their united forms—whether in Ardhanarishvara, the embodiment of masculinity and femininity in perfect harmony, or Harihara, the union of

destruction and preservation—they left humanity with profound lessons—though we have still not grasped them fully. Ardhanarishvara challenges our limited understanding of gender, reminding us that masculinity and femininity are not opposites but complementary forces that can coexist and even merge into a singular, balanced identity. It whispers to us that balance is not about highlighting differences but about embracing them to create something greater.

Harihara reminds us that even the most powerful entities can work together seamlessly, blending their identities to create something greater. It also proves that masculinity and femininity aren't just swappable; they can blend, merge, and exist together in one entity, proving that gender is way more fluid than we often think.

And here's the kicker: Both forms are still worshipped today, proving that ancient wisdom often outpaces modern understanding. So the next time someone insists gender roles are set in stone or pits opposites against each other in a futile argument, remember the divine duo—and maybe, just maybe, channel your inner Ardhanarishvara or Harihara. Embrace balance, merge perspectives, and if all else fails, invoke their stories to settle the debate with divine authority—and maybe even win that argument.

* * * * *

4

The Warrior Eunuch

Imagine this: you're a princess, the leading lady of your own fairy tale, poised to live happily ever after with your true love. Then, out of nowhere, your story gets hijacked by a meddling warrior who thinks kidnapping is a perfectly acceptable hobby. That, dear reader, is how Amba, the Princess of Kashi, found herself starring in a saga of thwarted love, burning revenge, and a plot twist involving gender transformation. Buckle up, because this tale is anything but predictable.

Once upon a time—because every good story starts like that— there was a grand *swayamvara* (you know, that traditional 'pick-your-hubby' ceremony) in the glittering halls of Kashi. Picture it: silk banners fluttering in the breeze, garlands of flowers draped everywhere, and a hall filled with eligible bachelors hoping to win the hearts of the three radiant princesses: Amba, Ambika, and Ambalika. Each sister was dressed in her bests, ready to size up the suitors and make her choice. For Amba, the stakes were particularly high—her heart already belonged to the dashing King of Salwa, and she planned to place her garland around his neck.

But life has a way of throwing curveballs, especially when Bhishma is involved.

Enter Bhishma: elder statesman of the Kuru dynasty, a warrior so formidable that armies shaked at the mere mention of his name. With a salt-and-pepper beard (*in my imagination, anyway*) and a vow of celibacy stronger than anyone's New Year resolutions, Bhishma showed up at the *swayamvara* uninvited. And not just to spectate— oh no. He stormed in, took one look at the scene, and decided the three princesses would make excellent brides for his half-brother, Vichitravirya. Because, apparently, nothing says "wedding goals" like abducting the entire bridal party.

Bhishma didn't just waltz up and ask politely. He crashed the party, fought off every protesting suitor, and swept the sisters onto his chariot like a man on a mission. Amba's plan to garland her beloved was replaced by a bumpy ride through chaos.

Now, Vichitravirya, to his credit, was probably just as surprised as everyone else. Bhishma dropped the sisters off like an Amazon delivery and announced, *"Here are your brides!"* Cue the awkward silence.

Amba, however, was not about to accept this turn of events. She gathered her courage, approached Vichitravirya, and spilled the tea: her heart belonged to King Salwa. To his credit, Vichitravirya, a decent guy in this saga, let her go. But here's the thing about fairy tales—they don't always follow the script.

Amba returned to King Salwa, hoping for a tearful reunion. Instead, she got a door slammed in her face. Salwa, nursing his bruised ego after being publicly upstaged by Bhishma, refused to take her back. *"You were kidnapped!"* he spat, as if that was somehow her fault. Talk about adding insult to injury.

Heartbroken and humiliated, Amba decided there was one person left to blame: Bhishma. She stormed back to the Kuru palace and demanded he take responsibility for the mess he'd made of her life. But Bhishma, steadfast in his vow of celibacy, refused. *"Sorry, not my problem,"* he essentially said, which was the final straw for Amba.

Fueled by a rage hotter than a thousand suns, she swore vengeance. She begged, pleaded, and schemed to rally kings to fight Bhishma. But here's the problem: Bhishma was practically an ancient superhero. No one dared challenge him. Frustrated but undeterred, Amba turned to the gods.

Enter Lord Shiva, the patron deity of dramatic revenge arcs. Amba's ardent prayers caught his attention, and he appeared before her and basically told her in a super casual tone, *"Revenge? Sure, but in your next life."*

Amba, never one to delay, immediately killed herself, securing her revenge saga's sequel in the next birth.

Fast-forward to Shikhandini, her reincarnation, born to King Drupada. Here's the twist: Drupada desperately needed a son to secure his dynasty, so when Shikhandini was born, he simply decided to raise her as a boy. Problem solved, right? Well, not quite.

Shikhandini grew up mastering the art of war, politics, and everything else a future king would need. Everyone treated her as a boy, and no one questioned it. Until, of course, the wedding night.

Shikhandini's bride, a princess with high expectations, quickly realized something was amiss. She tattled to her father, King Hiranyavarna, who flew into a rage and let's just say all hell broke loose. Feeling deceived, he declared war on Drupada's kingdom. Poor Shikhandini, caught in the mess, did what any self-respecting person would do in such a crisis: ran straight into the forest.

There, amidst the trees and moonlight, Shikhandini encountered a Yaksha—a supernatural being with a flair for the dramatic. Seeing her plight, the Yaksha offered a solution: *"Let's trade. I'll take your femininity, and you can have my masculinity. Temporarily, of course."* Talk about taking one for the team.

Desperate to save her reputation and kingdom, Shikhandini agreed. The Yaksha, true to his word, made the swap. And just like that, Shikhandini became Shikhandi—a man in body and spirit, ready to fulfill her destiny.

Sikhandini returned as Shikhandi, verified her masculinity, and sent King Hiranyavarna packing with his army. Crisis averted! But, of course, nothing is ever that simple. Kubera, the Yaksha's boss, wasn't thrilled about the sex swap shenanigans and cursed the Yaksha to remain female until Shikhandi's death. So, Shikhandini permanently became Shikhandi, completing her transformation.

Cut to the Kurukshetra war, where Shikhandi finally got her big moment on the battlefield of Kurukshetra, standing shoulder-to-shoulder with the Pandavas. On the tenth day, Arjuna hid behind her to shoot Bhishma. When Bhishma saw her, he froze. As a man bound by dharma, he couldn't fight someone born female. This hesitation proved fatal. Cue the dramatic volley of arrows, and boom—Bhishma was down, revenge was served hot, and Amba's arc finally closed.

Now, Shikhandi's story isn't just about revenge. It's about identity, resilience, and defying societal norms. Born a female, living as a male, and thriving as a warrior, Shikhandi challenges every box society tries to put her in. She even fathered

The Warrior Eunuch

a son—because why not? And let's be real—if anyone could pull off being a warrior, a royal, and a gender-fluid icon, it's Shikhandi…she still remains one of the fiercest, most complex characters in Indian mythology!

* * * * *

5

The Son of Two Gods

So, remember the time we talked about Harihara—the incredible fusion of Lord Shiva and Lord Vishnu? Well, guess what, this story takes us one step further—to their divine progeny, Lord Ayyappa. If you think your family dynamics are complicated, wait until you hear the story of Lord Ayyappa—a divine child born from two dads, raised as a prince, and destined to defeat a tigress-riding demoness. If there were ever a mythological reality show, this saga would take the grand prize.

Let's rewind to where it all began: after the fabulous Durga annihilated Mahishasura, his equally furious sister Mahishi decided to avenge him. Now, Mahishi wasn't your average demoness—she was as smart as she was scary. She went into full revenge mode, performing severe penance until Brahma himself showed up, probably thinking, *"Oh boy, here we go again."*

"Grant me a boon," Mahishi demanded, her eyes gleaming with the kind of overconfidence that screams "bad idea."

Brahma, bound by his cosmic customer service policy, nodded. *"What do you want?"*

Mahishi smirked, channeling her inner evil-genius. *"Make me invincible... unless I'm killed by a child born from the union of Lord Vishnu and Lord Shiva."*

Brahma blinked. *"Uh, okay."* Spoiler alert: this loophole would come back to haunt her.

With her bulletproof blessing and satisfied with her own brilliance, Mahishi unleashed chaos like an over-caffeinated toddler. She tore through the three worlds and wreaked havoc on Gods, sages, and mortals alike. All suffered under her tyranny as the temples crumpled, gurukuls were burned, and even the heavens were attacked. Helpless, the celestial beings finally called an emergency "Save the Universe" meeting and decided to appeal to Lord Shiva and Lord Vishnu for help.

The gods pleaded with the two supreme deities to unite their energies and bring forth the child destined to end Mahishi's reign of terror.

And here's where the celestial plot thickens. Enter Vishnu, the eternal strategist, who already had an ace up his divine sleeve—Mohini, his enchanting female avatar. Now, if you remember Mohini from the Samudra Manthan episode, she was the literal definition of distractingly beautiful. She had already enchanted the asuras during the churning of the ocean, tricking them with a wink and a smile, into handing over the nectar of immortality. This time, Mohini's role was even more pivotal.

When Mohini appeared, radiating ethereal charm, even the great ascetic Shiva, who normally couldn't care less about worldly attractions, went, "*Who's that?*"

He was so smitten that he pursued Mohini across the cosmos. But this wasn't just a game of celestial tag— it was the universe setting the stage for something extraordinary.

Their union wasn't your average candlelit dinner kind of romance. When Shiva and Mohini

combined their cosmic energies, something miraculous happened. A child was born—from Mohini's thighs. Yes, thighs. Because when you're a god, you do things differently.

And thus arrived Ayyappa, free from earthly constraints, and in his unique position as the son of two male deities.

The gods, knowing that Ayyappa needed to grow up in the mortal realm, placed him near the Pampa River, where King Rajashekhara of Pandalam found him. The king, who'd been praying for a child, saw the baby and thought, *"Finally, my Amazon Prime order came through!"* He adopted the boy and named him Manikananda, after the golden bell around his neck.

Manikananda grew up to be everything a king could wish for—brilliant, courageous, kind-hearted, and skilled in both warfare and governance. He was a protector of the weak, a wise counselor to the king, and a beloved figure among his people. But where there's divine perfection, there's always a jealous stepmother lurking in the background.

The queen, who had a biological son, wasn't thrilled about Manikananda potentially inheriting the throne. So, she did what any scheming character in a soap opera would do—she faked a terminal illness and declared that the only cure was tigress milk. *"Oh, and Manikananda should get it,"* she added, her voice dripping with fake innocence. A dangerous and seemingly impossible task, it was a calculated move to rid her of Manikananda.

But Manikananda wasn't one to back down. Off went Manikananda into the forest, calm as ever, probably thinking, *"This is gonna be a great story for the gods later."* Deep in the woods, he encountered none other than Mahishi herself. What followed was an epic battle straight out of a blockbuster movie.

For days, the earth trembled as Manikananda and Mahishi clashed. Mahishi, boosted by her Brahma-approved invincibility clause, fought like a demon possessed (literally). But Manikananda, with his divine lineage, was unstoppable. In the end, Mahishi fell, and the universe breathed a collective sigh of relief.

But Manikananda didn't just stop there. Nope—he went the extra mile. He milked the tigress (because why not?) and then rode back into the kingdom on her back.

Let's pause here to appreciate this visual: a teenage boy, casually riding a tigress, probably waving at the stunned villagers like it was just another Tuesday.

When he returned, the queen was too stunned to speak (probably thinking, "Didn't see that coming."). The king, the people, and the gods all gathered as the truth about Manikananda's divine origins was revealed.

At that moment, Manikananda's mortal identity as the adopted prince of Pandalam gave way to his cosmic identity as *Hariharaputhiran*—the son of the two supreme deities. As the gods praised him, the people began to address him with a new name: *Ayyappa*, derived from the Tamil/Malayalam term "Ayyan," meaning "respected father" or "lord." This name was a reflection of the reverence he commanded and his divine legacy.

Realizing Ayyappa's divinity, the king and queen begged him to take the throne. But the transition from Manikananda to Ayyappa also marked his spiritual evolution. While Manikananda was the beloved son and prince of Pandalam, Ayyappa was the eternal guardian of dharma.

Realizing this, Ayyappa declined the throne. Instead, he chose the path of asceticism, retreating to the tranquil forests of Sabarimala. There, he meditated, his presence transforming the hill into a sacred site.

Today, the temple of Sabarimala in Kerala is one of India's most renowned pilgrimage sites. Every year, millions of devotees clad in simple black clothing, undertake a challenging journey.

They observe strict discipline and follow an aesthetic life days before the pilgrimage to purify themselves and be worthy to honor Lord Ayyappa, who represents the triumph of good over evil, devotion, and harmony.

What's more, the temple is a beacon of unity, welcoming all irrespective of caste, creed, or religion—a reflection of Ayyappa's inclusive origins.

Being the child of two male deities, he challenges traditional notions and symbolizes unity in diversity.

Ayyappa's story is proof that when the universe wants something done, it doesn't care about your "impossible" checklist—it'll throw in some magical matchmaking, thigh-born miracles, and a tigress for good measure.

That's the magic of mythology: a chaotic mix of gods, demons, and drama that somehow leaves you with a weirdly comforting message— everything's gonna be okay, even if it takes a celestial-level plot twist!

*   *   *   *   *

6

A Tale of Alternating Identities

Imagine a love story that starts with a divine prank and evolves into a cosmic masterpiece. This isn't your standard boy meets girl, they fall in love tale—this love story that defies every norm—a tale where identity isn't fixed, love isn't defined, and acceptance is the only constant—this is the story of Ila and Budh, an epic from ancient Indian mythology that feels startlingly modern. It could even be a headline of a TED Talk on love and the art of breaking the rules.

But before we talk about Ila and Budh, let's rewind to Sudyumna, the protagonist who kicked this off. Sudyumna was your quintessential dashing prince—brave, charming, and always ready for adventure. He was the kind of guy who didn't read the fine print on heavenly warnings and would gallop into danger without asking questions, which, in hindsight, might have been his biggest flaw.

One day, during a hunting trip, Sudyumna and his entourage wandered into a forest. The air shimmered with a godly stillness, the trees whispered secrets only the gods could hear, and flowers bloomed in colors not found on any mortal palette. The place was so magical it practically screamed, *"Turn back now, or else!"*

But Sudyumna, being the *"or else"* kind of guy, didn't. The thing is this wasn't just any forest—it was Parvati's private sanctuary, a divine retreat created with one very specific rule: *No boys allowed*. Shiva, ever the loving husband, had cast a spell ensuring that any man who entered would instantly transform into a woman. Sudyumna, blissfully unaware of this enchanted no-entry sign, strolled right in.

The magic hit him like a cosmic makeover montage. In the blink of an eye, his princely armor hung loose on a woman's frame, his jawline softened, and his reflection in the river belonged to someone else entirely. Gone was Sudyumna, the prince; in his place stood Ila, a woman so stunning that the flowers in the forest probably started blushing.

Now, imagine his—sorry, her—reaction. Imagine the shock. One minute, Sudyumna was a prince with a kingdom and a mission; the next, Ila was grappling with questions like, *"What just happened? Who am I now?"* It was a cosmic identity crisis wrapped in a gender-bending twist. Becoming Ila wasn't just a physical transformation; it was a seismic shift in identity. Imagine one moment being a dashing prince with an army and a kingdom to rule, and the next, grappling with losing everything you knew—your name, identity, even your gender. How do you come to terms with something like that?

At first, Ila did what anyone would do—panic, mourn the loss of Sudyumna, and maybe curse a few gods. But here's the thing about Ila: resilience ran in her veins. Over time, she began to embrace her new reality, discovering that femininity wasn't a weakness but another form of strength. She wasn't just surviving—she was thriving, blending the courage of Sudyumna with the grace of Ila.

Ila's existence became a lesson in duality: strength and vulnerability, masculine and feminine, loss and acceptance.

The gods, of course, were watching all this unfold, likely amused and ready to place bets on what would happen next.

Just when Ila thought she had reached the limits of life's surprises, the stars had other plans—literally. Enter *Budh*, the celestial god of Mercury. With his silver tongue, intellect sharper than a blade, and an aura that radiated charm, Budh was like a comet streaking into Ila's life.

Here's the thing about Budh: he didn't care about societal norms or the external labels attached to Ila. He wasn't interested in her past as Sudyumna or in societal norms that tried to box people into rigid roles. He saw Ila, a soul who had endured more twists and turns than a season finale of Game of Thrones and emerged more radiant for it. Budh fell in love not with a man or a woman but with the person Ila had become—a complex, beautiful blend of experiences, a soul filled with resilience and grace. Their connection was instant, a bond deeper than gender or form. Budh didn't just fall for Ila; he crashed into love, the kind that turns worlds upside down and rewrites destinies.

Their union was not just romantic; it was symbolic—a godly message that love transcends all boundaries, even those between male and female. Their bond was built on mutual respect, a deep understanding of each other's journeys, and a shared ability to laugh in the face of cosmic absurdity.

With time, their love bore fruit in the form of a son, Pururavas, who would grow up to become one of the most legendary kings in Indian mythology. Pururavas carried forward the legacy of his parents—a blend of divine power, human resilience, and the courage to defy norms.

But even as Ila and Budh celebrated their life together, Ila couldn't ignore a lingering longing—the desire to reclaim her identity as Sudyumna. She wanted balance, stability, and the chance to honor both aspects of herself.

Determined to find a resolution, Ila approached Lord Shiva and Goddess Parvati. In a heartfelt plea, Ila explained her struggle. "*Look,*" she said,

"I've been a prince, a woman, a lover, and a parent. Can I just be all combined and not live between the two worlds…?" She wanted the freedom to be both Sudyumna and Ila, without losing herself in the process.

Moved by her honesty, the divine couple came up with a solution that could only exist in mythology: Ila would alternate between her identities. For one month, she'd be Sudyumna, the prince. The next, she'd be Ila, the woman. It wasn't perfect, but it was enough to honor both identities and give Ila some control over her life.

And here's where the story truly shines. This heavenly solution brought a new dimension to Budh and Ila's relationship. Budh didn't just accept this arrangement—he embraced it. Every month, he adapted to Ila's shifting identities, proving that love isn't about what's on the outside but about the connection between two souls. Sometimes he loved Sudyumna, the brave prince; other times, he loved Ila, the graceful woman. But always, he loved the essence of who they were.

What might have been a challenge for lesser beings became a testament to their bond. Their

relationship wasn't about rigid roles but about adaptability, acceptance, and an unshakable understanding of each other.

So, the next time someone tells you love has rules, tell them about Ila and Budh. Ila and Budh's story is more than just a love story—it's a celebration of fluidity, acceptance, and the boundless nature of love. It reminds us that identity is not fixed, love doesn't follow a script, and the heart doesn't care about labels.

In a world obsessed with rules and definitions, Ila and Budh's tale feels refreshingly modern, showing us that the greatest love stories aren't the ones that fit neatly into boxes but the ones that break free of them entirely.

* * * * *

7

A Love That Lives On

Remember Kurukshetra? That wasn't just a battlefield; it was mythology's version of an epic Netflix series. Heroes, villains, drama, cosmic interventions—it had everything.

Amid the chaos of this battlefield stood Aravan, a hero whose story is equal parts epic and tragic. Aravan wasn't just some random guy on the battlefield; he was Arjuna's son. And not just any son—he was the product of Arjuna's brief but dramatic fling with Ulupi, a Naga princess. Their story began during Arjuna's exile, which was essentially a road trip where he collected wives like trading cards. Ulupi, who ruled an underwater kingdom beneath the Ganga, spotted him one day and thought, *"Yep, that's the one."*

Using her mystical powers, she pulled Arjuna into her aquatic Airbnb. Once there, she wasted no time. *"Look,"* she said, *"I'm deeply in love with you, and also, we're destined to have a son who'll be a hero. What do you say?"* Arjuna, ever the Kshatriya with a knack for saying yes to destiny (and, let's be honest, a beautiful woman), agreed. They spent one memorable night together before he swam back to his questing life, leaving behind a son destined for greatness—and an awkward post-breakup dynamic.

Their son, Aravan, grew up to be the warrior you'd expect from a union of a Pandava and a Naga princess: brave, noble, and just a little bit magical. But even heroes can't escape the fine print of destiny. When the Pandavas needed divine intervention to win Kurukshetra, the gods demanded a sacrifice. Not just any sacrifice—one that required a hero's blood. Cue Aravan, who stepped up like it was no big deal.

But this is no ordinary tale of war and valor. This is again a love story—a love that defied time, gender, and societal norms.

So the story gets juicy here. Before Aravan got ready to lay down his life, he had one very human request: he wanted to get married. *"If I'm going to die tomorrow,"* he thought, *"I at least want to experience love today."* Call it hormones, call it the pursuit of romance, or just call it good old FOMO—Aravan wasn't going to die without ticking "marriage" off his bucket list.

There was just one problem: who would marry him? Most women aren't thrilled about becoming a widow the morning after their wedding. His wish seemed doomed until Krishna, ever the cosmic wingman, stepped in. Krishna, deeply moved by Aravan's plight, decided to grant the young warrior his wish in the only way possible.

Now, Krishna didn't just solve problems; he turned them into legendary stories. Transforming into Mohini, his female form so enchanting it could make the gods themselves do a double take, Krishna appeared before Aravan. And let me tell you, Mohini didn't just show up; she slayed.

Her beauty was so dazzling it could launch a thousand weddings, and Aravan was no exception. He fell head over heels, and soon enough, they were married in a ceremony that was equal parts joyous and bittersweet.

For one day and night, Aravan lived the life he'd dreamed of. Mohini, ever the devoted partner, made sure he felt loved, cherished, and, well, let's just say completely satisfied. She essentially ensured that he got the emotional (and sexual) closure, he sought before his sacrifice.

This wasn't just a union of God and mortal; it went beyond physical or emotional connection— it was a divine statement about the fluidity of identity and the boundless nature of love. Mohini's transformation wasn't merely a disguise; it was an affirmation that love could transcend the confines of form and gender.

When dawn broke, Aravan met his fate with the courage of a hero. And Mohini, now a widow, mourned him with a grief so intense it left even the gods misty-eyed. Her sorrow wasn't just about losing a partner; it was about the universal pain of saying goodbye too soon.

But the story doesn't end there. Aravan's sacrifice and Mohini's gesture of love didn't just fade into legend. They found new life in Tamil Nadu's *Koothandavar Festival*. This vibrant annual celebration isn't just a nod to mythology; it's a dazzling, colorful affirmation of identity and inclusion.

Every year, transgender women, known as the *Aravanis*, gather to honor Aravan by symbolically marrying him. They dress as brides, adorning themselves in vibrant saris and intricate jewelry, and participate in ceremonies that are equal parts celebratory and sacred. For one day, they revel in love and validation, finding acceptance in a tradition that sees them not as outsiders but as central to a divine narrative.

For them, Aravan isn't just a simple mythological figure; he's a patron of their community, a deity who accepts and celebrates them for who they are.

And just like Aravan's story, the festival is layered. When the ceremonies end, the Aravanis mourn Aravan's symbolic death, mirroring Mohini's grief. It's a moment that encapsulates the bittersweet reality of love—joy and loss, celebration and sorrow, all wrapped into one beautiful, messy package.

Aravan and Mohini's story reminds us that love is as much about acceptance as it is about connection.

Their union may have been fleeting, but its impact is eternal.

Aravan and Mohini's tale isn't just about gods and warriors; it's a story about the power of love to transcend boundaries—of time, gender, and even mortality. Their union, fleeting as it was, left a legacy that continues to inspire and empower.

And now for the ultimate takeaway: From Aravan's ultimate sacrifice to Mohini's profound gesture of love, this story is proof that love doesn't fit neatly into boxes. So, the next time someone tries to define love with rigid rules or confine identity to labels, drop this story on them.

Because, honestly, if a god can turn into a goddess, marry a mortal for a day, and inspire a festival that celebrates inclusion centuries later, then surely love isn't here to follow anyone's rulebook. It's here to rewrite them entirely.

* * * * *

To Those Who Made This Possible

This book is the result of countless cups of *chai*, hours of pouring over ancient texts, and the unwavering patience of my loved ones. First, I have to thank my late grandmother, who introduced me to mythology the same way she introduced me to pickles—with love, wisdom, and a little bit of spice. Her knack for spinning mythological tales over lazy afternoons planted the seed for my obsession with these stories, and her influence shaped the foundation of this book.

I also owe a great deal to the ancient texts themselves—*Skanda Purana, Brihadaranyaka Upanishad, Bhagavat Purana, Vishnu Purana, Mahabharata, Rig Veda, Matsya Purana, Shiva*

Purana, and more. They've been my guide, my challenge, and my constant reminder that ancient India was far more progressive (and occasionally outrageous) than we give it credit for.

My husband, Manoj, has been my pillar of support through it all—patiently listening, encouraging, and standing by me through every high and low of this journey. Whether it was lending an ear or pretending to be deeply fascinated during dinner conversations, he was there every step of the way.

Special thanks to the moms (both mine and his), who not only tolerated my ramblings about gender fluidity in mythology but wholeheartedly supported me through the chaos.

A heartfelt shoutout to my boys, Ruven and Raghav. Thank you for letting me step away from being "Mom" long enough to chase this dream. It was Ruven's publishing triumph that finally lit the fire under me to finish this book and share these stories. This book wouldn't exist without you both—and I promise I'll make up for all those hours I spent with my nose buried in ancient manuscripts instead of playing with you.

And finally, to my inner circle of friends, who kept me motivated in their own unique ways—Shivraj, for his constant ramblings about writing a book (which, I must say, were both entertaining and oddly reassuring), Mandar, for reading my drafts with patience and providing thoughtful insights, and my sister Aakriti, for being my first critic, editor, and unofficial book therapist. Your support, honesty, and occasional tough love helped shape this book into what it is. A huge shoutout to Neha, Shilpi, Rita, Disha, Vidya, and Divya for their unwavering support, laughter, and reality checks. Whether indulging my book rants or just being your wonderful selves, you made this journey all the more special.

Last but not the least, a big thanks to Sukanya from Notion Press for all her help in getting my book published. Her support and guidance made the whole process so much easier, and I'm really grateful for her hard work in bringing my vision to life.

To everyone who's helped along the way, directly or indirectly: this book is as much yours as it is mine. Thank you for making this journey unforgettable.

Who Wrote This Anyway?

*P*riyanka *is an instructional designer by day, a storyteller by heart, and a full-time juggler of two boisterous boys. Armed with a degree in English Literature and a background in journalism, she has spent her life writing everything from instructional content to sticky notes reminding her kids to do their homework.*

Her obsession with mythology began as a curious fascination and quickly spiraled into a love affair with ancient tales that are far more dramatic than any soap opera.

When she's not decoding the mysteries of the Mahabharata or sneaking in chapters of her favorite books, you'll find her trying to outsmart her kids in word games (often unsuccessfully). Through this book, Priyanka seeks to shine a spotlight on the queer stories woven into ancient mythology, reminding us that the spectrum of gender and love is as old as time itself.